For Jose, Issa, and Max. —AH

For Evie, Thomas, and Amelia. —NS

First published in the United States in 2023 by Sourcebooks

Text © 2023 by Alice Hemming
Illustrations © 2023 by Nicola Slater

Sourcebooks and the colophon are registered trademarks of Sourcebooks.

The sketches and full color art were created in Photoshop, with the occasional scanned paint or graphite texture added here and there.

Published by Sourcebooks Jabberwocky, an imprint of Sourcebooks Kids
P.O. Box 4410, Naperville, Illinois 60567-4410
(630) 961-3900
sourcebookskids.com

Originally published in 2023 in the UK by Scholastic Children's Books, a division of Scholastic Ltd.

Cataloging-in-Publication Data is on file with the Library of Congress.

Source of Production: C&C Offset Printing
Date of Production: October 2022
Run Number: 5027658

Printed and bound in China.
CC 10 9 8 7 6 5 4 3 2 1

DON'T TOUCH THAT FLOWER!

Alice Hemming   Nicola Slater

sourcebooks
jabberwocky

"Hello brand new day.
Hello sunshine.
Hello lovely leaves!
Nice to see you back."

"Squirrel, **I** know you love this flower, but it doesn't **really** belong to you."

WHAT? Then **whose** flower is it?

"That bee over there was EATING my flower! Can you BELIEVE IT?"

"No, Squirrel, the bee was collecting nectar. It's good for the flower and the bee."

The morning after that...

"GO AWAY! Shoo!"

"What are you doing now?"

"What are you doing **this time?**"

"I don't want my flower to get wet."

"But it needs water to grow. Your flower needs a shower!"

"Of course it does! Silly me!"

The next morning...

"Then you're right, I do like spring! And, Bird, the flower is growing in between your tree and my tree...but it's a bit closer to my tree, so it's MY flower, isn't it?"

...I suppose it is, Squirrel.

"Oh, Bird—look at this!
It's a new flower, and it's
small and yellow and perfect.
It looks like the sun!"

New flowers are another
sign of spring, Squirrel.

"Well, *it* sounds like you heard a cuckoo call and a bumblebee buzz and saw a swallow. Those are all signs that spring has arrived."

"Spring...
Do we *like* spring?"

"Yes, of course."

"Bird!"

Yes, Squirrel? What is it?

"It's getting very BUSY, Bird.
There was a sound like CUCKOO
and one like BUZZZ and a bird with a
strange tail nearly flapped into my eye!"

CUC-KOO!

"Wait—what was that?"

BUZZZ!

"And WHAT was THAT?"

"Your flower is a wildflower...

It's there for **everyone** to enjoy."

"Still, I'm **not** taking any chances.

In fact, I'll keep my flower safe under here."

"Oh dear, Squirrel."

"Will it survive?"

"I hope so, but you need to give it some air and light and space."

That night...

"What have I done?
I hope my flower is all right.
I'm not going to sleep a wink."

But instantly...

ZZZZZZZZZZZZZZZ.

The next morning...

"WOW, Bird!

WOW!

Where did they all come from?"

Our Flowers

"Flowers don't really belong to us."

As Squirrel found out, wildflowers belong to us all. It can be fun to look
for flowers growing outside in the wild. You can enjoy them,
take photos, and draw them. When you start looking, you will find
flowers growing in all sorts of places.

Flowers are living things

"Your flower needs a shower!"

A flower is part of a plant and plants need the same sorts of things as
people do to live and grow. They need light, water, air, and food. They don't
eat like we do, though. They make their food using energy from the sun.

Flowers attract pollinators

"That bee over there was EATING my flower."

In the story, the bee was collecting nectar to make into honey.
Bees also gather pollen, which they spread to other plants as they travel
from flower to flower. This helps the plants grow. Bees are *pollinators*.
Butterflies, other insects, some birds, and some bats can also be pollinators,
and flowers look and smell beautiful to attract them.